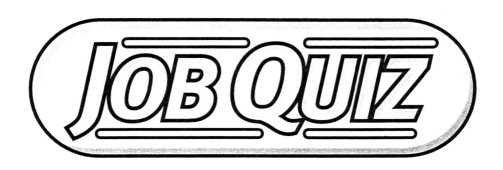

ACTIVITIES FOR CAREERS EDUCATION

Tony Crowley

Job Quiz

ISBN 1 902876 24 5
© Copyright Lifetime Careers Wiltshire 2001.

Lifetime Careers Wiltshire, 7 Ascot Court,
White Horse Business Park, Trowbridge BA14 0XA
Tel: 01225 716023
Fax: 01225 716025
E-mail sales@wiltshire.lifetime-careers, co.uk

Design and layout by Shane Feeney
Printed by Avon Printing, Melksham, Wilts

Contents

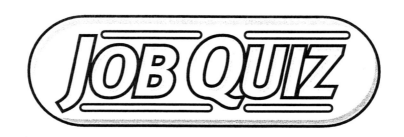

Introduction

Welcome to the Job Quiz Book. It will help you to widen your knowledge about different jobs through puzzles, pictures, riddles and questionnaires.

Use your school or college careers library to find the answers. There are clues or hints in the form of two or three letters (e.g. IC, YAD, etc) with a lot of the questions. These are codes from the CLCI (Careers Library Classification Index) and most careers libraries use this system for filing careers information. You will also find references to a card system called Signposts which may be available in the careers library.

Why not try some of the quizzes on your family or friends and test their job knowledge too? The answers will be found at the back of the book.

We hope the job Quiz Book will encourage you to explore the information in your school careers library and to seek the help of your careers teacher or careers adviser.

Match of the Day

A quiz for football fans. Can you match up the nicknames below with these football teams? The nicknames give an idea of the type of work in the areas where the teams first played.

Grimsby Town	(a) Steelmen
Motherwell	(b) Gunners
Luton Town	(c) Toffeemen
Reading	(d) Glaziers
Arsenal	(e) Cobblers
Barnsley	(f) Hatters
Crystal Palace	(g) Biscuitmen
Everton	(h) Mariners
Northampton Town	(i) Colliers
Rotherham	(j) Millers

Thwaaack!

Wordsearch

In this book, there are 20 quizzes based on the groups in the Signposts careers information cards. One word from the name of each group has been hidden in the panel below. For example, BUILDING is in the third line from the bottom. The twenty words run forwards, backwards, up, down and diagonally. As you find them, place their names next to their Signposts code letter. For example, BUILDING will go next to the letter C.

```
Y  E  N  G  I  N  E  E  R  I  N  G  O  P
B  N  A  S  D  H  K  R  I  N  S  N  I  Q
Z  V  D  J  L  I  E  H  E  L  P  I  N  G
C  I  T  S  I  T  R  A  J  P  R  L  F  N
B  R  C  S  H  J  I  C  L  U  Y  L  O  I
S  O  C  L  S  D  P  T  U  T  N  E  R  S
R  N  M  A  E  C  L  I  J  B  H  S  M  I
E  M  V  M  T  I  I  V  A  D  U  B  A  N
B  E  P  I  J  R  S  E  X  Z  W  S  T  A
M  N  H  N  K  T  K  U  N  D  E  R  I  G
U  T  R  A  N  S  P  O  R  T  C  D  O  R
N  A  S  F  N  L  J  Q  C  E  I  W  N  O
A  B  U  I  L  D  I  N  G  M  F  F  M  Z
R  Y  O  A  M  C  S  U  D  G  F  T  I  Y
P  L  W  S  R  E  T  U  P  M  O  C  A  C
```

Code		Code	
A	....	K	....
B	....	L	....
C	....	M	....
D	....	N	....
E	....	O	....
F	....	P	....
G	....	Q	....
H	....	R	....
I	....	S	....
J	....	T	....

What do you know about Active and Physical work?

(Signposts A)

1. Name two physically-active jobs beginning with the letter C that are usually found in a social club, a public hall, a church or a school.

2. Which two sciences might a firefighter find very useful? (Clue: MAF)

3. On an oil rig, what is the difference between a roughneck and a roustabout? (Clue: ROB)

4. What is a cradle and who might use one? (Clue: UF)

5. Why would a fence erector use an auger?

   (a) to dig a hole (b) to tighten wire (c) to hold up a post (d) to pacify a bull

6. Which is the odd one out?

   (a) bill poster (b) aerial rigger (c) steeplejack

   (d) road worker (e) demolition worker

7. What would a fisherman or fisherwoman be doing when 'shooting' ?

   (a) firing a harpoon (b) setting out nets (b) towing lines

   (c) pulling in the fish (d) boasting about a catch

8. On average, how many bins or containers does a refuse collector empty each day?

   (a) 100 (b) 200 (c) 300 (d) 400 (e) 500

9. What is the name of a job that involves humping heavy equipment at a gig? (Clue: GAD)

10. *Be forceful* and sort out this scrambled job title:

    IF I FLAB

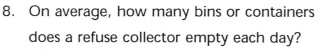

Harps and arrows

In the year 2000, Health and Safety officials warned the government that the sound of military bands and gunfire broke the 1989 Noise at Work Regulations and could damage soldiers' hearing. The Ministry of Defence has set up a working party to investigate the problem and suggest some practical solutions.

White Christmas

Every Christmas, Luis Guzman, a Puerto Rican businessman, buys thousands of tons of snow from a town in Canada. He transports it back home by freezer ship to San Juan where he charges families $30 a day to play in the snow, sledge, make snowmen and throw snowballs.

What do you know about Artistic and Creative work?

(Signposts B)

1. Which is the odd one out?

   (a) hairdresser (b) make-up artist (c) beauty therapist (d) beauty consultant

2. Therapists help people to cope with, or recover from, illnesses.

   Name two kinds of therapy which use artistic and creative skills. (Clue: JOD)

3. In what type of work might you find someone jiggering and jollying?

   (a) belly dancing (b) making pottery (c) drawing cartoons (d) massaging

4. What is the difference between a print finisher and a bookbinder? (Clue: SAR)

5. What do you call someone who produces the words in advertisements?

   (a) copywriter (b) spin doctor (c) adsmith (d) publicist

6. Websites are often designed by specialist designers, but who else might perform this kind of work? (Clue: ED)

7. What occupation is represented by the organisation RIBA?

8. What does a 3-D designer do? (Clue: EG)

   (a) makes virtual reality images (b) designs objects

   (c) designs pop-up cards (d) designs typefaces

9. Most people in the advertising business work in London. TRUE or FALSE?

10. *Refocus* this scrambled job title:

    HO GROPER PATH.

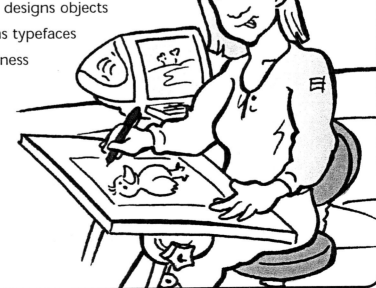

Quick Crossword

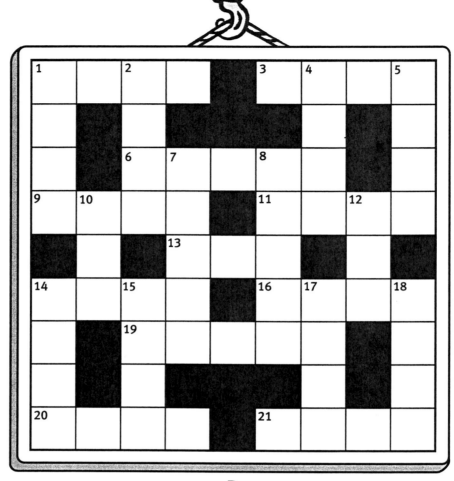

Across

1. May be collected by the bus driver. (4)
3. Felixstowe is an important one. (4)
6. People carrier: wood shaper. (5)
9. A solicitor would do this for a client. (4)
11. Someone in 17 down might join one. (4)
13. A title that may be demanded at work. (3)
14. Held by a fashion model. (4)
16. A busy time for a sales assistant? (4)
19. A town job requiring a loud voice. (5)
20. Filled at a forecourt. (4)
21. Needs the right pressure. (4)

Down

1. An unsuccessful recording or show? (4)
2. Secures a ship to its mooring. (4)
4. To call up a computer file. (4)
5. To colour or dye hair. (4)
7. A powerful beam of light. (5)
8. A job requiring patience and patients. (5)
10. Are good leaders born under this sign? (3)
12. Feeling like this? See a doctor. (3)
14. Letters: a job. (4)
15. To search the horizon: an X-ray. (4)
17. The largest of the Armed Services (4)
18. A cutting tool needs a sharp one.

What do you know about Building and Construction?

(Signposts C)

1. What is a 'hod' and who would use one?

2. Job title: What T works with ceramics, stone or marble and uses grout?

3. What are the normal entry qualifications for training as a building technician?

4. Stonemasons cut and prepare stone for building and monuments, but what is the difference between a banker mason and a fixer mason?

5. Name a job responsible for working out the costs of a building project. (Clue: UM)

6. In the construction industry, there are more electricians than painters and decorators. TRUE or FALSE?

7. On a building site, what does a clerk of the works do? (Clue: UD)
   (a) organise a trade union (b) guard the site (c) inspect the work

8. What would a carpenter mean by 'shuttering' ?
   (a) boarding up an empty house   (b) fixing shutters to windows
   (c) making a mould for concrete   (c) straightening bent nails

9. In a building project, who would be responsible for planning things like lighting, heating, electrics and plumbing? (Clue: UJ)
   (a) construction manager   (c) building control surveyor
   (b) building services engineer   (d) construction plant mechanic

10. Can you *see through* this scrambled job title? ZEALRIG

Multi-skilled MacSporran

From the Job Quiz Book (1976): *On the island of Gigha in Scotland, one man, Seamus MacSporran, performs all the following jobs: coastguard, garage attendant, constable, sub-postmaster, taxi driver, pier master, shipping agent, school bus driver, general merchant, public lavatory attendant, registrar, ambulance driver, undertaker, delivery man and rent collector. He also runs the island's guest house and used to be the postman but was made redundant.* **Twenty five years on and we hear that Seamus has just retired but the Job Quiz Book keeps going!**

Good News-Bad News

During a week of chaos on Britain's rail services, an information assistant at a Cambridgeshire station worked flat out to handle 10,846 enquiries. Unfortunately, every caller wanted to know what was happening and he was unable to provide a useful answer.

What do you know about Communicating Information and ideas?

(Signposts D)

1. What do you call someone who assembles the lists found at the back of books?

   (a) compiler (b) lexicographer (c) tabulator (d) indexer (Clue: FAD)

2. What kind of a job is a P.R.O? (Clue: OG)

3. What are barristers called in Scotland?

   (a) briefs (b) attorneys (c) counsellors (d) advocates

4. Who works in a call centre?

5. Copy editors and sub-editors prepare text for publication,

   but what is the difference between these two jobs? (Clue: FAD)

6. In how many modern foreign languages must an interpreter be fluent? (Clue: FAL)

7. What do you call someone who teaches English to those who do not

   speak it as their first language? (Clue: FAB)

8. There are three kinds of air traffic controller: area, approach, and aerodrome.

   Which one communicates with an aircraft during its flight? (Clue: YAB)

9. Can you *reinterpret* this scrambled job title? ART OR SLANT

Figures of Speech

Here are some traditional expressions which have a link with work.

Do you know what they mean?

1. To be in the same boat.
2. To corner the market.
3. To play second fiddle.
4. To go under the hammer.
5. To sling one's hook.
6. To be a jack of all trades.
7. To clear the decks.
8. To hit the nail on the head.
9. To rest on one's oars.
10. To strike while the iron's hot.
11. To pay the piper.
12. To put up the shutters.
13. To take the reins.
14. To know the ropes.
15. To sail close to the wind.
16. To talk shop.
17. To steal a march on (someone).
18. To keep a weather eye open.
19. To be tarred with the same brush.
20. To cook someone's goose.

Nightmare

Here is a new version of an old riddle. Some see the solution immediately, whereas others puzzle over it for hours - even days. A few sad people never solve it.

One night, at a call centre, two operators were on duty. While one was making tea in the rest room, the other sat at his screen waiting for the next call. To pass the time, he was reading a book about the French Revolution. After a while, his eyes felt heavy and he became sleepy. Gradually, his head sank lower and lower until it was almost resting on the screen in front of him and he fell asleep. In his dream, he imagined he was living in Paris at the time of the revolution and was on his way to the guillotine to the jeers of a large and violent crowd. Struggling desperately for his life, he was dragged up the steps to the platform and his neck laid across the fatal plank. Stricken with absolute terror, he stared at the large basket of heads in front of him and awaited the falling blade.

At that moment, with the tea brewed, the other operator came out of the rest room. Seeing her colleague asleep, she walked across to him and tapped him smartly on the back of his neck with a teaspoon. 'Wake up!' she called, 'Tea's ready.'

The sleeping operator fell dead at his post!

The problem: Although such an awful ending is possible, what evidence does the story contain which proves that it cannot have happened?

Higher Education Quiz

1. How many universities are there in the United Kingdom?.
   (a) 63 (b) 82 (c) 96 (d) 205

2. Recent changes in higher education mean that all degree courses are now concentrated in the universities.
   TRUE or FALSE?

3. Applications for most degree, HND and DipHE courses have to be made through the Universities and Colleges Admissions Service (UCAS).
   TRUE or FALSE?

4. Applications to UCAS that are received after mid-January are automatically rejected.
   TRUE or FALSE?

5. Applicants for university must list a choice of six courses.
   TRUE or FALSE?

6. Students who pass one A-level (or Scottish Higher grade) can consider studying for a Higher National Diploma or a Diploma in Higher Education.
   TRUE or FALSE?

7. You receive a conditional offer stating two Bs and a C but later obtain grades A, C and D. What are your chances of being accepted?
   (a) Very good, as the same number of points were obtained.
   (b) It is difficult to say, it depends on the other applicants' results.
   (c) Not good, you must get the exact grades stated or higher.

8. The entry qualifications required for a course reflect its
   (a) quality (b) difficulty (c) popularity

9. If courses in different institutions have exactly the same name, this indicates that they are very similar in content.
   TRUE or FALSE?

10. Under the UCAS system, how many offers can an applicant hold while awaiting exam results?
(a) 1 (b) 2 (c) 3 (d) 4 (e) 5

11. Many institutions now offer places without interviewing the applicants.
TRUE or FALSE?

12. All students must make an annual contribution to the cost of a course.
TRUE or FALSE?

13. Applications for student loans must be made at the start of the academic year.
TRUE or FALSE?

14. Student loans are means-tested.
TRUE or FALSE?

15. Student loans are repaid in instalments after a graduate earns a salary of
(a) £10,000   (b) £15,000 (c) £20,000

16. EU students are charged the same fees as UK students.
TRUE or FALSE?

17. An accelerated degree course is half the length of a normal course.
TRUE or FALSE?

18. A thin sandwich course usually contains:
(a) one long placement (b) several short placements
(c) a mixture of long and short placements?

19. In offering a sandwich course, the college or university must guarantee to find students work placements.
TRUE or FALSE?

20. Entry requirements are generally lower for mathematics, physical sciences and engineering courses.
TRUE or FALSE?

What do you know about Engineering?

(Signposts E)

1. Name a type of engineering beginning with the letter A. (Clue: RAB)

2. What would an engineer mean by 'CAD'?

    (a) Central assembly department   (b) Completely automatic device

    (c) Can anyone draw?   (d) Computer-aided design

3. What engineer beginning with H might be responsible for a traffic calming scheme? (Clue: UN)

4. Toolmakers make things like hammers, chisels and screwdrivers. TRUE or FALSE?

5. Both work with metal but what is the difference between a sheet metal worker and a plater?

6. What does a clinical engineer do?

    (a) Designs medical equipment   (b) Checks the quality of products

    (c) Purifies sewage   (d) Monitors air conditioning systems

7. Which of the following employ maritime (or marine) engineers?

    (a) Royal Navy   (b) Merchant Navy

    (c) oil and gas exploration companies   (d) shipbuilders

8. What is the difference between an electrical engineer and an electronic engineer?

9. What type of engineer designs construction projects like roads, bridges or dams?

10. Can you *repair* this scrambled job title? MEAN CHIC

Open all hours

One in four of the working population in the United Kingdom works between six at night and six in the morning

Newspeak

People at work have always developed new words or phrases to communicate information quickly to other workers. Sometimes these become part of our everyday speech (like E-mail) or they sound ridiculous (like Careerquake) and are soon forgotten. Here are a few words or phrases you might hear at work. Do you know what they mean? Which ones will still be around when you retire?

1. human resources ....
2. buying an idea ....
3. a raft ....
4. coming onstream ....
5. downsizing ....
6. challenge ....
7. soft skills ....
8. a take ....
9. mission statement ....
10. tracking ....
11. footfall ....
12. a sea-change ....
13. interfacing ....
14. telecommuter ....
15. portfolio ....
16. acting up ....
17. upskilling ....
18. ringfencing ....
19. the cutting edge ....
20. a brand ....

Groupies

a medley of folk singers

a ring of jewellers

a shower of forecasters

a bevy of publicans

a round of bartenders

a school of caretakers

a string of guitarists

a battery of bouncers

a handful of masseurs

a bunch of florists

a body of undertakers

a clique of photographers

a layer of carpet fitters

Can you think of any more?

....

....

What do you know about health and medicine?

(Signposts F) Careers Library Section J

1. Acupuncturists are employed by the National Health Service.

    TRUE or FALSE? (Clue: JOD)

2. Paediatrics refers to the treatment of

    (a) the elderly (b) children (c) feet (d) urinary problems

3. Name a job which provides treatment for those suffering from back trouble.

    (Clue: JOD)

4. What is the difference between a dental technician and a dental hygienist?

5. Both an orthotist and a prosthetist work with people who have disabling

    conditions, but which one would fit an artificial limb? (Clue: JOL)

6. How long does training to be a doctor take?

    (a) 3 - 4 years (b) 5 - 6 years (c) 7 - 8 years (Clue: JAB)

7. What job helps people recovering from an illness to develop

    confidence and cope with everyday tasks?

8. Where might an occupational health nurse be employed? (Clue: JAD)

9. Both ophthalmic opticians and orthoptists test eyesight,

    but what else do orthoptists do? (Clue: JAL)

10. *Chew over* this scrambled job title:

    AINT I TIED

Joined up talking

'In Fe, after COA, I can do an NVQ in IT by FMA
under an NTO for an ILA. O.K.?'

'And how about a course in joined-up talking?'

According to the Industrial Society, the happiest workers in Britain today are dinner ladies. And the least satisfied? Call centre workers. There are 400,000 of them - more workers than the coal, steel and vehicle production industries put together. They earn £9,000 a year less than the average salary and enjoy some of the worst working conditions in Britain.

What do you know about Helping People?

(Signposts G)

1. In which job would you welcome people to a business, answer their questions, answer the phone and take messages? (Clue: CAT)

2. In general, it is quite difficult to find training as a funeral director. TRUE or FALSE? (Clue: IP)

3. Here are some older job titles. What do we call them now?

    (a) Youth employment officers (b) Truant officers (c) Almoners

4. What is the difference between a childminder and a nursery nurse? (Clue: See KEB)

5. Can you spot the odd one out?

    (a) air steward/ess (b) nurse (c) probation officer (d) prison officer

6. By law, all counsellors must be properly qualified. TRUE or FALSE? (Clue: KEK)

7. What does an equal opportunities officer do?

8. Job title: What C describes a priest or minister who works in a university, a prison, a factory, or the Armed Forces?

9. If people are homeless, where should they first go for help?

    (a) police station (b) social services office

    (c) housing department or association

    (d) Citizens' Advice Bureau

10. Can you *look after* this scrambled job title? ANDREW

How good a salesperson are you?

1. You are serving a customer in a clothes shop. There are three dresses which she likes and which fit her quite well, but she cannot decide which one to buy. Would you...
   (a) suggest that she bought all three as one dress won't last all that long anyway?
   (b) advise her to go home and think about it?
   (c) try to find out why she cannot decide?
   (d) get her to try another dress?

2. You are trying to interest home owners in a new system of double glazing. At your first call, the occupier tells you that he is very busy and cannot leave the task he is doing to hear about your system. Would you...
   (a) apologise for disturbing him and leave as quickly as possible?
   (b) ask if you may call on another occasion?
   (c) stick your foot in the doorway and describe the system as quickly as you can?
   (d) suggest that you describe it to his partner?

3. Your shop carries several computer printers but a customer asks about a model which you do not usually stock. Would you...
   (a) explain that you do not have that particular model in stock, but offer to show some which have similar facilities?
   (b) outline the limitations of the model requested and highlight the advantages of some of the printers in stock?
   (c) simply announce that the printer is not available at your shop?
   (d) offer to phone several shops in the neighbourhood to see if they might have it in stock?

4. You are arranging the window display of a leather goods shop in order to attract customers into the shop. Would you...
   (a) fill the window with cheaper items to give the impression that your shop has bargain prices?
   (b) avoid pricing most of the goods you display so that customers will have to come inside the shop to ask?
   (c) make an eye-catching display of just one beautifully-designed and expensive item?
   (d) display a variety of goods from the cheapest to the more expensive items?

5. Working in a shoe shop you know that many customers have one foot slightly larger than the other. A lady customer complains that all the left foot shoes she has tried appear to be rather tight. Would you.....
   (a) advise her to purchase two pairs of shoes - one slightly larger than the other - to ensure a perfect fit?
   (b) explain that all shoes in stock are of a high quality and perfectly matched?
   (c) suggest that she tries another size as her right foot may be a little smaller than her left?
   (d) suggest that she tries a larger size as her left foot appears to be too big.

6. A customer asks to see an item which has been placed in the centre of a window display and will be awkward to remove. As it is the only one in stock, would you......
   (a) ask the customer to go back outside and take another look to make sure it is what he really wants?
   (b) remove the item from the display as carefully as possible?
   (c) remove the item but show that you are going to a lot of trouble in doing so?
   (d) suggest that the customer calls back tomorrow when the item will have been removed from the window for a change of display?

7. You are serving in the fancy goods section of a department store. A customer has picked up the same vase several times from a mobile display unit. Your supervisor has moaned about people messing up this particular display. Would you.......
   (a) offer to find a similar vase for inspection from stock?
   (b) draw the customer's attention to the 'please do not handle' notice near-by?
   (c) call loudly for the supervisor?
   (d) wheel the display unit out of the customer's reach?

8. You are just about to wrap a shirt which a customer has purchased. Which of the following might be worth saying?
   (a) 'Anything else, Sir?'
   (b) 'Not bad for the time of year, is it?'
   (c) 'Would you like some new underwear?'
   (d) 'How about a nice tie to go with the shirt?'

9. Your customer thinks she might get a particular television model a little cheaper elsewhere. Would you...
   (a) politely show her to the door?
   (b) point out that what she saves on the price she will probably spend in shoe leather searching around?
   (c) explain why you think the price you are asking is quite reasonable?
   (d) impress on her that when the set breaks down your repair service is second to none?

10. You are reluctant to take an older car in part exchange for a newer model as it is rather scruffy and may not be too easy to sell. Would you...
   (a) explain to the customer that you can afford to be fussy as you have built up a reputation for good vehicles?
   (b) suggest that the customer sells the vehicle privately and offer a few tips on how this might be done?
   (c) jot down the names of nearby scrap merchants on one of your sales cards and hand it to the customer?
   (d) reject the car and impress upon the owner the dangers of driving a rusty vehicle?

What do you know about Law and Security?

(Signposts H) Careers Library Section L, M

1. To be a prison governor, experience as a prison officer is essential.
    TRUE or FALSE? (Clue: MAD)

2. In which job might you be checking 'landing cards' ?
    (a) lift tester (b) air traffic controller (c) parachute instructor
    (d) immigration officer

3. In what job do you inspect businesses to make sure that traders
    are not breaking the law? (Clue: COP)

4. No qualifications are required to work as a private investigator.
    TRUE or FALSE? (Clue: MAG)

5. In what type of work would you check various public places to ensure
    they are safe and healthy? (Clue: COP)

6. In a magistrate's court, who calls witnesses and gets them to swear on
    oath to tell the truth?
    (a) an usher (b) an oaths clerk (c) a registrar (d) a lackey (Clue: LAG)

7. Which job requires the higher qualifications?
    A court clerk or a court administrative officer? (Clue: LAG)

8. Most local authorities do not allow women to
    work as nightclub bouncers.
    TRUE or FALSE?

9. In the past 25 years, which of the following
    occupations has seen a threefold increase in numbers?
    (a) probation officers (b) police
    (c) prison officers   (d) lawyers

10. Help *rescue* this scrambled job title:
    OUR CAD STAG

Writing on the wall

Scrawled on a wall in West London:
'What's the worst job you ever had?'
Underneath was written
'Cleaning off your graffiti'

A to Z

Although there are something like 20,000 different jobs, you only need to list 26 of them here - each one starting with a different letter of the alphabet. The figure in brackets is the score you receive for each job title. Good luck with X!

A ....(2)

B ....(3)

C ....(1)

D ....(2)

E ....(3)

F ....(3)

G ....(4)

H ....(4)

I ....(4)

J ....(5)

K ....(5)

L ....(4)

M ....(2)

N ....(4)

O ....(4)

P ....(2)

Q ....(5)

R ....(3)

S ....(2)

T ....(2)

U ....(5)

V ....(5)

W ....(4)

X ....(6)

Y ....(5)

Z ....(5)

Your total score ....

15 of these 24 work words are misspelled. Can you find and correct them?

1. manufacture
2. adress
3. imformation
4. superviser
5. accident
6. comittee
7. attendance
8. aplicant

9. eficiency
10. tempory
11. reciept
12. decision
13. personel
14. punctual
15. benifit
16. computor

17. factory
18. requirment
19. tennant
20. occured
21. cancel
22. dissmis
23. enterprise
24. consistant

What's my line?

I need a licence to perform this work.
My pockets are sewn up and I wear no rings.
I work late into the night.
I am supervised by a 'pit boss'.
What am I?

What do you know about Leisure, Tourism and Food?

(Signposts I)

1. Name a job which involves both administrative and sporting skills. (Clue: GAG)

2. Whose work involves split tins and bloomers?

3. Name two jobs directly concerned with helping tourists. (Clue: GAX)

4. In an hotel, what is the chef below the head chef normally called?

    (a) second chef (b) assistant chef (c) deputy chef (d) junior head chef (Clue: IB)

5. What is the minimum age for serving customers at a bar?

6. There are no longer any height restrictions on air cabin crew.
   TRUE or FALSE? (Clue: YAB)

7. Name a job that might pamper you with a pedicure.

8. If training to provide silver service, would a waiter or waitress be

    (a) laying out an attractive buffet

    (b) arranging food on silver plates

    (c) cooking at the side of the customer's table

    (d) serving at the table from separate dishes?

9. Apart from receptionist and manager, can you name four other jobs found
   in an hotel? (Clue: IB)

10. *Sober up* this scrambled job title: PAIN CLUB

What do you know about Media and Entertainment?

(Signposts J)

1. What might an actor mean by 'resting'?

2. Who might be found working under the direction of a choreographer?

3. In a television studio, what name is usually given to the person who passes instructions from the director to the performers or presenter?

4. Which profession is represented by the union Equity?

   (a) actors (b) models (c) musicians (d) jockeys

5. Which are the two most requested sizes for female models?

   (a) 8 (b) 10 (c) 12 (d) 14 (e) 16

6. Wannabees often send their tapes to the A & R department of record companies. What do these initials stand for?

7. What might a production assistant mean by 'continuity work'?

8. What percentage of media studies graduates find some kind of employment. in that field.

   (a) 40% (b) 55% (c) 60% (d) 75% (e) 90%

9. Opportunities for entertainment managers are restricted to just a few areas of the country.

   TRUE or FALSE?

10. Can you *tune up* this scrambled job title?   CAN I MIS U

Believe it or not

Since 1998, the number of Elvis Presley impersonators around the world has doubled each year. If this rate of increase continues, it is estimated that by the year 2020, one third of the world's population will be impersonating Elvis for a living.

Spot the Errors

Can you spot the ten safety errors in this busy office?

Odd Links

Can you work out the odd connection between these pairs of jobs?

1. A tennis umpire and a swimming pool lifeguard ....
2. A racecourse bookie and an orchestra conductor ....
3. A pastry cook and a dental surgery assistant...
4. A word processor operator and a concert pianist ....
5. A carpet fitter and a priest ....
6. A firefighter and a disc jockey ....
7. A Formula One driver and a bill poster ....
8. A dentist and a saw doctor ....
9. A grave digger and an ear piercer ....
10. A Justice of the Peace and a worker expecting a baby ....

'Do you have any unusual talents to offer?'
'Oh yes, I have won prizes for completing crosswords.'
'Well, we were thinking of something you might perform at work.'
'But this was at work.'

Sorry!

Standing by a paper-shredding machine with an important-looking document, a new employee in a Sheffield office asked a passing clerk how to operate it. 'No problem, luv' she replied, taking the paper from him. Just put it in here and press the button.' The new man thanked her and then asked 'And how do I make more than one copy?'

What do you know about office work?

(Signposts K)

1. Why would an office keep a supply of 'petty cash' ?
2. Job titles. What S goes with medical, bilingual, legal, school or farm? (Clue: CAT)
3. For what kind of an organisation might a grants officer work?
4. What is the difference between a typist and a word processor operator? (Clue: CAT)
5. In the world of business, what do the initials PA stand for? (Clue: CAT)

    (a) private account (b) personality assessment (c) personal assistant
6. What kind of work does a company secretary perform? (Clue: CAP)
7. In what type of office might you find a settler working alongside an investigator? (Clue: NAG)
8. What do you call someone who helps a solicitor to draw up wills, issue writs and prepare court cases? (Clue: LAD)
9. In the next few years, the number of people employed in high street banks is expected to

    (a) increase (b) stay much the same (c) decrease (Clue: NAD)
10. *Organise* this scrambled job title: RACE TYRES

Good News-Bad News

According to a national survey of secretaries, 50% of bosses forget appointments and family birthdays, 36% never say 'thank you', 22% swear out loud, 14% chain smoke, and 6% are extremely scruffy. The good news is that 30% of those secretaries who attempted to change their bosses behaviour were successful.

Interests Quiz

Plant and care for trees, shrubs or house plants	3 2 1 0	Drive a tractor or a harvester on a farm 3 2 1 0
Exerclse animals at a kennel or a stable	3 2 1 0	Look after the wildlife in a safari park 3 2 1 0
Search for oil, natural gas or valuable minerals	3 2 1 0	Inspect sunken wrecks and salvage cargoes 3 2 1 0
Pilot a civilian or military aircraft	3 2 1 0	Maintain engines and machinery on a ship 3 2 1 0
Build an airstrip in a jungle or forest clearing	3 2 1 0	Help to construct roads, bridges or tunnels 3 2 1 0
Assemble wind or solar-powered machinery	3 2 1 0	Design and assemble miniature computers 3 2 1 0

Settle disputes between firms and customers	3 2 1 0	Speak on behalf of defendants in court 3 2 1 0
Demonstrate security equipment at an exhibition	3 2 1 0	Sell buildings, land or antiques by auction 3 2 1 0
Sell holidays and tours in a travel agency	3 2 1 0	Persuade people to take out insurance policies 3 2 1 0
Be responsible for recruiting and rejecting staff	3 2 1 0	Organise a team of security guards 3 2 1 0
Question suspects or witnesses and make arrests	3 2 1 0	Supervise young offenders on probation 3 2 1 0
Describe important events on radio or television	3 2 1 0	Explain political policies to voters 3 2 1 0

Develop drugs to combat serious diseases	3 2 1 0	Research the side effects of medicines and drugs 3 2 1 0
Research medical problems affecting animals	3 2 1 0	Collect and study different forms of marine life 3 2 1 0
Analyse and test food grown on the ocean bed	3 2 1 0	Improve the crops of developing nations 3 2 1 0
Explore methods of predicting earthquakes	3 2 1 0	Study weather patterns to predict storms 3 2 1 0
Develop ways of improving safety in vehicles	3 2 1 0	Develop and test satellite navigation systems 3 2 1 0
Design psychological tests for staff selection	3 2 1 0	Investigate links between television and violence 3 2 1 0

Value life and property for insurance policies	3 2 1 0	Calculate the costs of an unusual project 3 2 1 0
Study stocks and shares for investors	3 2 1 0	Check secret bank accounts for fraud 3 2 1 0
Compile tables of data from research projects	3 2 1 0	Interpret fashion statistics and predict sales 3 2 1 0
Prepare documents for committee meetings	3 2 1 0	Compile papers for cases in the High Court 3 2 1 0
Keep records of sales at an auction	3 2 1 0	Select and catalogue books for a library 3 2 1 0
Check town plans for land development	3 2 1 0	Prepare maps from aerial surveys 3 2 1 0

Compose classical or popular music	3 2 1 0	Sing and play with a group of musicians 3 2 1 0
Act serious or comedy roles in films or on TV	3 2 1 0	Perform mime, dance routines or ballet 3 2 1 0
Produce illustrations for a publisher	3 2 1 0	Plan the artwork for a sales brochure 3 2 1 0
Design unusual fashions for men or women	3 2 1 0	Create a new range of furniture 3 2 1 0
Create individual hairstyles in a salon	3 2 1 0	Prepare exotic dishes for banquets 3 2 1 0
Write short 'jingles' to advertise a product	3 2 1 0	Report on local events for a newspaper 3 2 1 0

Plan community activities for disabled people	3 2 1 0	Advise and help people with hearing difficulties 3 2 1 0
Nurse and care for elderly people	3 2 1 0	Give assistance to mothers in childbirth 3 2 1 0
Help young people with severe speech disorders	3 2 1 0	Provide therapy sessions for hospital patients 3 2 1 0
Organise activities and games in a playgroup	3 2 1 0	Care for young children in a community home 3 2 1 0
Teach games to children with special needs	3 2 1 0	Teach one or more subjects in a school or college 3 2 1 0
Be a counsellor in a Citizen's Advice Bureau	3 2 1 0	Give support and advice to homeless families 3 2 1 0

Activity	Score			
Grow crops on a wasteland or smallholding	3 2 1 0			
Train dogs to detect narcotics	3 2 1 0			
Survey tunnels and shafts in a disused mine	3 2 1 0			
Test drive a high-speed passenger train	3 2 1 0			P/A
Build a sports hall and leisure complex	3 2 1 0			
Rebuild or repair racing-car engines	3 2 1 0			

Negotiate wage deals with employers	3 2 1 0
Persuade people to buy a new range of cosmetics	3 2 1 0
Encourage businesses to advertise their products	3 2 1 0
Manage a large hotel, club or restaurant	3 2 1 0
Help keep law and order in a tough district	3 2 1 0
Interpret at conferences or business conventions	3 2 1 0

E/P

Test samples of blood and human tissue	3 2 1 0
Discover new methods of improving livestock	3 2 1 0
Explore ways of removing radioactivity from soil	3 2 1 0
Develop wind, wave or solar energy systems	3 2 1 0
Devise experiments to test plastics or rubber	3 2 1 0
Find ways of reducing stress at work	3 2 1 0

S/I

Prepare bills of quantities from architects' plans	3 2 1 0
Audit accounts and sort out tax problems	3 2 1 0
Develop computer programs to analyse statistics	3 2 1 0
Improve the wording and layout of official forms	3 2 1 0
Update files in a hospital records department	3 2 1 0
Compile route maps or instructions for travellers	3 2 1 0

C/A

Play records to entertain radio listeners	3 2 1 0
Tell amusing stories and jokes to an audience	3 2 1 0
Select photographs for a popular magazine	3 2 1 0
Design and paint murals from freehand drawings	3 2 1 0
Embroider motifs on furnishings or clothes	3 2 1 0
Write poetry, short stories or novels	3 2 1 0

A/C

Help people with limited sight to become mobile	3 2 1 0
Advise and treat patients at a health centre	3 2 1 0
Restore the injured to health by exercises	3 2 1 0
Find foster homes for children	3 2 1 0
Train unemployed people for new jobs	3 2 1 0
Help school-leavers in choosing a career	3 2 1 0

S/S

Here is a quiz with a difference. There are no right or wrong answers - just the answers you care to give.

Instructions: Read through these lists carefully. Look at each item and place a circle around the score to show how you rate it.

3 = I would **really like** to do this.
2 = I think I **might like** this.
1 = I am **not too sure** that I would like this.
0 = I would **definitely avoid** this.

????

When you have graded all the activities, look back at those to which you gave a score of 2 or 3. Read them again and put a circle around the word in each item that made it seem interesting. Then read the scoring instructions in the answers.

What do you know about Organising Information and People?

(Signposts L)

1. Which one of these might a human resources officer perform?

    (a) researching transport and housing needs (b) recruiting company staff

    (c) running a sewage works (d) distributing aid in a disaster   (Clue: CAS)

2. What kind of a qualification is an MBA?

3. Health service managers are only employed by the National Health Service. TRUE or FALSE?

4. How many different careers are open to officers in the RAF?

    (a) 4 (b) 11 (c) 19 (d) 30 (Clue: BAL)

5. In the Army, what role is played by the Supporting Arms? (Clue: BAF)

6. In the Merchant Navy, you can train to be a deck officer, an engineer officer, or both. TRUE or FALSE? (Clue: YAL)

7. Where might you find a practice manager at work? (Clue: CAL)

8. What is a gavel and who might use one?

9. What kind of a manager gets materials, goods or supplies moved to where they are needed? (Clue: Y)

10. *Reorganize* this scrambled job title:

    I DAMN TRAITORS

In a survey of occupational health risks, publicans, seafarers, bar staff and hotel managers were top of the list. School helpers, ministers of religion and nurses were at the bottom. What do you think the study was about?

Crystal balls

In 1979, a team of researchers at a univerity in Ireland predicted that, by the year 2001, petrol-driven cars would have disappeared from the roads, secretaries would no longer be required in offices, and that children would have stopped watching television.

What do you know about Scientific and Technical work?

(Signposts M)

1. What school subject is often called 'the language of scientists' ?
2. Whose work might involve finding where it is safe to place an oil rig?

    (a) a hydrographer (b) a marine biologist (c) an oceanographer (Clue: UM)
3. What kind of materials testing is known as NDT for short?
4. Name two jobs which study events in the sky or in space? (Clue: QOF)
5. What is the difference between a food scientist and a food technologist? (Clue: QON)
6. In industry, what do the initials R & D stand for?
7. What type of work is covered by a forensic scientist?

    (Clue: QOT)
8. Which of the following might develop new drugs for humans and animals?

    (a) microbiologists (b) chemists (c) pharmacologists
9. What kind of an inspector tests raw materials and finished products to see if they are of the right standard? (Clue: SOZ)
10. *Find some life* in this scrambled job title:

    BIG STOOL

We aim to miss

Mission statements are the aims or goals of an organisation and are often dressed up to impress the public. This pompous example is one of my favourites.

Our aim is for customers to experience our continuing commitment to excellence through the provision of quality information that encourages personal fulfillment in harmony with the environment.

Check out your local Careers Service's mission statement. It might be even better!

Crossword

Clues Across

6. This job may involve fashion, sports, crime, weddings etc (12)
8. Vendors: traders (7)
9. A body of troops (5)
10. To correct a piece of text (4)
12. Entertains with body movements (6)
14. To ruin or damage goods (5)
15. Visitors to an hotel (6)
16. To restore to health (4)
19. A retaken exam (5)
21. A mill where thin layers of steel are made (7)
22. Shows others how to make or operate things (12)

Clues down

1. A colliery (4,4)
2. One reason for working (5)
3. The newspapers (5)
4. A particular branch of the police service (7)
5. Tools or work clothes (slang) (4)
6. Customers at 14 down (10)
7. Studies the stars without a telescope (10)
11. The UK association for psychologists (initials) (3)
12. An archaeologist may be found working here (3)
13. Get your prescription from them
14. A stop on a railway line (7)
17. A collapse on the stock market (5)
18. An office worker (5)
20. Brought an action against someone in court (4)

What do you know about Selling and Shopwork?

(Signposts N)

1. How old must you be to sell wine?

   (a) 16 (b) 17 (c) 18 (d) 19 (e) 20 (f) 21

2. What kind of a dealer might sell you something that has been 'distressed'? (Clue: FAG)

3. Name three places where a car hire receptionist might work.

4. What is meant by a 'hot shelf' in a supermarket?

   (a) a shelf containing freshly cooked food

   (b) a display at the entrance to the store

   (c) a display at normal eye height

   (d) a shelf containing expensive spirits

5. Where in the high street might you find a negotiator at work? (Clue: UM)

6. What is a 'franchisee'?

7. What kind of shopping is often referred to as e-tailing?

8. What would a salesperson mean by 'cold calling' ?

9. Which three of these sales words have been misspelled?

   (a) wholesaler   (d) reciept

   (b) comercial   (e) commission

   (c) catalogue   (f) advertisment

10. Try *redistributing* this scrambled job title.

    I MEND ARCHES

Puzzler 2

Napoleon Bonaparte once called the English a nation of

(a) sailors (b) smallholders (c) sausage makers (d) shopkeepers (e) scoundrels?

What do you know about Environmental work?

(Signposts O)

1. What do you call someone who prunes branches and removes damaged or diseased trees?

    (a) tree doctor (b) tree lopper (c) tree stripper (d) tree surgeon (Clue: WAF)

2. What is the difference between a countryside ranger and a countryside officer?

3. What is 'landfill' ?

    (a) a method of burying waste   (b) reclaimed land

    (c) a system for repairing pot holes   (d) a foundation for buildings

4. What kind work is covered by amenity horticulture? (Clue: WAD)

5. What is a rotavator and who might use one?

6. Does an arboriculturalist manage the growing of trees for their appearance or for their timber?

7. What would an environmental engineer mean by 'renewable energy' ?

8. Why does the Environment Agency employ hydrometry officers?

    (a) to measure waves, tides and currents

    (b) to predict flash flooding

    (c) to monitor and manage water resources

    (d) to investigate plant and animal life in the ocean

9. What is the difference between sewage and sewerage?

10. *Change the appearance* of this scrambled job title: SLAP CAR END

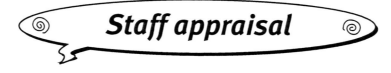

Staff appraisal

The annual staff evaluation can sometimes bring out the worst in managers:

'He should go far, and the sooner he starts, the better.'

'She brings much joy whenever she leaves the room.'

'This employee is depriving a village of an idiot.'

'He has this gift for making strangers immediately.'

'The wheel is still turning, but the hamster is dead.'

Interview Quiz

Pick up some useful interview tips by completing this poem with the help of the list of missing words below.

I arrived at Smith's office with minutes to ....

making sure the receptionist knew I was ....

I took my CV - that's a page of key ....

and a few deep breaths to help me ....

When they .... out my name, I said in my ....

Sparkle! Go for it! Words of that ....

My handshake was firm, my appearance quite ....

I knew I was off to a promising ....

The .... which came in a regular ....

I answered with more than a 'Yes' or a ....

They seemed quite impressed with my knowledge of ....

Well they didn't sell books and had never made ....

"And now is there something you'd like to ......'

So I checked .... first and holidays ....

' We think you're the person we've been looking ....

to sit at this desk with your name on that ....'

'But I only .... for a very small ....'

' No, this is for .... When can you ....'

'And then I awoke for a voice that I ....

'Get up! You're late for your job ....'

door	flow	relax	knew	called
ask	interview	there	mind	questions
for	crisps	spare	smart	manager
applied	facts	start	last	Smiths
training	part	No	kind	start

33

Mechanic: 'I've reassembled the engine.'

Garage manager: 'Good. I hope you didn't lose any parts.'

Mechanic: 'No. In fact, there are some left over.'

What do you know about Transport and Driving?

(Signposts P)

1. What is the minimum age to become an approved driving instructor?

   (a) 17 (b) 18 (c) 20 (d) 21 (e) 25 (Clue: YAD)

2. Apart from driving, name two other skills or qualities required by a chauffeur.

3. What would a taxi driver mean by 'the knowledge' ?

4. All traffic wardens are employed by the police. TRUE or FALSE? (Clue: MAZ)

5. Driving skills: spot the odd job out.

   (a) train driver (b) tractor driver (c) bus driver (d) lift truck driver

6. Who might be found consulting Glass's Guide and why?

7. At what age can you train to be a truck driver? (Clue: YAD)

   (a) 17 (b) 18 (c) 19 (d) 20 (e) 21

8. In speaking to a controller, what would a motorcycle courier mean by POB?

   (a) I have a parcel of books (b) I have a passenger on the back

   (c) I have package on board (d) I have police organising a breathalyser

9. Are you allowed to drive between applying for and receiving a provisional licence? YES or NO?

10. Can you land this scrambled vehicle?
    CHEER PILOT

Puzzler 3

What do a bishop, a motorcycle messenger, a food packer, a traffic warden, a building site worker, and a surgeon all have in common?

Yesterday's jobs

Here are some tools and equipment that were used about 150 years ago.
Can you work out what they were used for and by whom?

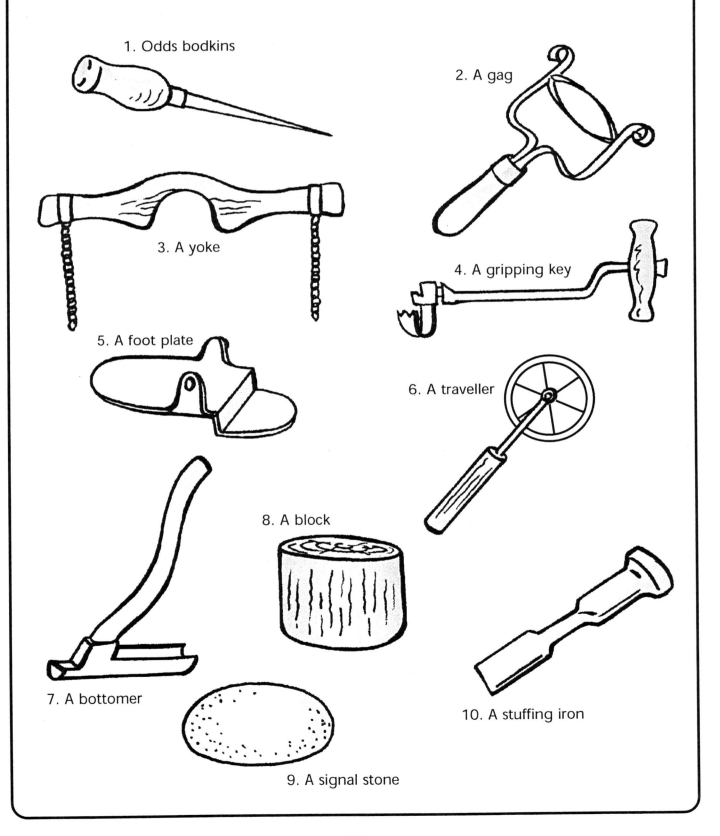

1. Odds bodkins

2. A gag

3. A yoke

4. A gripping key

5. A foot plate

6. A traveller

7. A bottomer

8. A block

9. A signal stone

10. A stuffing iron

Barking mad

520 postmen or women are seriously bitten each year by dogs. One gas inspector makes a note of homes with unfriendly dogs by writing against the address: 'meter reader eater'.

What do you know about work with Animals?

(Signposts Q)

1. What do you call a hairdresser for dogs? (Clue: WAM)
2. How many full-time gamekeepers work in Britain? (Clue: WAM)
    (a) 1000 (b) 3000 (c) 5000 (d) 8000
3. RSPCA or SSPCA inspectors must be able to swim.
    TRUE or FALSE? (Clue: WAL)
4. What kind of horse racing is called National Hunt?
5. People who exercise racing greyhounds have to run quite fast.
    TRUE or FALSE?
6. What do you call someone who fits horses with new shoes?
    (a) hoofer (b) shodder (c) tacker (d) farrier (e) hackster (Clue: WAM)
7. What is the correct name for a ratcatcher? (Clue: IJ)
8. What kind of a farmer checks oxygen levels, hatches eggs and traps weeds? (Clue: WAG)
9. Name three organisations which employ dog handlers.
10. *Muck out* the scrambled job title:
    HALT SAD BEN

Sorry!

During a firefighters' strike, an elderly lady summoned an army unit to release her cat which was trapped up a tree. After the job was done, she invited the team in for a cup of tea. Suitably refreshed, they backed their vehicle down her drive to the applause of onlookers, but accidently ran over and killed the cat.

Rights and Responsibilities

Here is a list of employment rights and responsibilities for young workers in most jobs. Four of these items are incorrect. Tick the real ones?

Rights

☐ 1. A written statement describing your conditions of service.

☐ 2. A minimum wage

☐ 3. Pay slip showing wages and deductions

☐ 4. Wages paid in cash

☐ 5. Four weeks paid leave each year

☐ 6. A working week limited to an average of 48 hours

☐ 7. Night work limited to an average of eight hours

☐ 8. Two days off work each week

☐ 9. 12 hours rest between each working day

☐ 10. 30 minutes rest if working for more than four and a half hours

☐ 11. A safe and healthy workplace

☐ 12. A medical assessment if working between 10.00 pm and 6.00 am

☐ 13. Freedom to belong to a trade union

☐ 14. Redundancy payments

☐ 15. Equal rights for men and women on career opportunities, training etc.

☐ 16. An agreed amount of notice if being dismissed

☐ 17. A reference when leaving

Responsibilities

☐ 18. To perform the job with care and skill

☐ 19. To work honestly

☐ 20. To obey all your employer's orders

☐ 21. To be loyal to your employer - even after you have left

☐ 22. To give the agreed amount of notice of leaving

Enterprise

During a fortnight's work experience at a printing company, Adam Hughes, a 17 year old student from Liverpool, designed an e-commerce system which secured contracts worth $1 million and saved the company from bankruptcy. Though offered a job in the USA branch of the company, Adam decided to pursue his dream of becoming an architect.

What do you know about work with Computers?

(Signposts R)

1. In computing, what is meant by 'hardware'? (Clue: CAV)

2. What term is often used to describe a computer failure?

3. What do the initials IT stand for?

4. Which of the following job titles is used to describe someone who writes advanced computer programs?
   (a) program developer (b) systems writer
   (c) software engineer   (d) computer nerd

5. What is the difference between a bug and a virus?

6. Job title: What S...A... designs a computer-based procedure to manage business problems?

7. What kind of program stores lots of information.

8. Can you name any health problems that are sometimes caused by using computers or visual display units?

9. What is the difference between a website designer and a webmaster?

10. *Debug* this computer workplace (one word): KELP SHED

Believe it or not

One well known Japanese firm has an unusual way of caring for employees when they are off work through illness. A personnel officer makes a home visit with a box of chocolates (for men) or a bunch of flowers (for women). The firm sees it as an act of concern and good staff relations. The workers' union describes it as 'barbaric intimidation'.

Job Satisfactions

Recently, a thousand workers were asked to rank the the following job satisfactions in order of importance. Which were the top and bottom five for men and women? How do you rank them? Will your ideas change with time? The results of the survey are presented in the answers.

Your choice

1. Making use of my talents and abilities ....
2. Working for a successful organisation ....
3. Perks and fringe benefits ....
4. Good basic pay ....
5. Opportunities for promotion ....
6. Job security ....
7. A strong trade union ....
8. An interesting and enjoyable job ....
9. Having a say in what goes on ....
10. Clean and safe working conditions ....
11. Managers who know their jobs ....
12. Flexible working hours ....
13. Not too many problems ....
14. Appreciation for doing a good job ....
15. Good equipment for doing the job ....
16. The chance to develop new skills ....
17. Working with people I respect ....
18. Doing something worthwhile ....
19. Working for an ambitious company ....
20. Having my complaints listened to ....
21. Opportunities for overtime ....

	Men	Women
Top five	....	....
Bottom five	....	....

What do you know about work with Numbers?

(Signposts S)

1. Once they were called wages clerks, but what are they called now? (Clue: CAT)

2. What time of the year might a book-keeper find rather stressful?

3. Job title: What B looks after the finances of a large school or college?

4. An actuary　(a) buys and sells stocks and shares

   (b) works out insurance risks and premiums

   (c) prepares a firm's accounts

   (d) invests money for a charity　(Clue: NAJ)

5. Where would a quantity surveyor be found working?

   (a) a construction project　(b) an engineering firm

   (c) a tax office　(d) a pharmaceutical firm　(Clue: UM)

6. Apart from abroad, where there seem to be quite a lot of them, where else might you find foreign clerks at work?　(Clue: NAD)

7. Most economists are employed by　(a) the banks

   (b) the newspapers

   (c) the universities

   (d) the government　(Clue: QOK)

8. Does a revenue officer work for a local council or an income tax office?　(Clue: CAB)

9. Job title: What A independently checks the accounts of companies?

10. Can you *figure out* this scrambled job title?
    I STAIN ATTICS

Good News-Bad News

'The good news is that we find you dynamic, punctual, efficient, honest, hard-working, loyal, and enthusiastic.' 'So what's the bad news?'
'Well, you are making the other employees very, very nervous'

A recent study of 1000 workers by London Guildhall University found that slim, attractive and tall people earn 13% more than average. A similar study in Iceland produced the same result and also found that brown haired people earned 10% more than blondes.

What do you know about working with your Hands?

(Signposts T)

1. The place where a sailmaker works is called a

   (a) cellar (b) kitchen (c) store (d) loft

2. Which is the odd one out?

   (a) pattern grader (b) pattern cutter (c) pattern maker

3. A piano tuner must be a skilled pianist. TRUE or FALSE? (Clue: GAD)

4. Where might you find glory holes, blowpipes and servitors?

   (a) an orchestra (b) a glassworks (c) an oil rig (d) an organ makers

5. What traditional furniture polishing skill has a European country

   in its job title? (Clue: SAJ)

6. What do you call a person who makes decorative metalwork such as wrought

   iron gates and railings? (Clue: SAW)

7. If you heard a tailor talking about 'cabbage', what would this be?

   (a) left-over material (b) lazy assistants (c) a tailor's dummy (d) coarse cloth

8. In which job would you find kneekickers and grippers being used?

   (a) weaving (b) carpet fitting (c) antique repairing (d) riot policing

9. Which job involves cutting and stitching leather or hides to make handbags,

   harnesses and bridles? (Clue: SAW)

10. Can you *recover* this scrambled job title? HOTEL PURSER

Survival

Each year more than 600 people are killed at work,
30,000 have major accidents, and 500,000 suffer injuries.

1. A workmate has burnt her arm on a steam pipe. Do you
    (a) cover the burn with grease   (b) flush it with clean cold water
    (c) bandage it tightly   (d) burst any blisters?

2. Whilst operating an electrical machine, a workmate receives a shock and
    is now lying in contact with the equipment. If possible, do you
    (a) pull him away as quickly as possible   (b) run for help
    (c) push him away with a piece of wood   (d) switch off the current?

3. Someone has swallowed poison and needs help. What would you do first?
    (a) check that her mouth is empty   (b) make her sick
    (c) give her a glass of water or milk   (d) dial 999 for assistance?

4. You are left looking after someone who is lying in a state of shock. Do you
    (a) keep him cold   (b) keep him talking
    (c) keep him warm   (d) keep him walking?

5. In assisting an unconscious casualty, first aiders often refer to the ABC of life.
    What do these letters stand for?

6. Your boss is sitting by a pile of broken glass with blood pouring from a cut
    'It's nothing serious,' he reassures you, 'but help me put a bandage on it.'
    What must you do first?

7. What do these
    symbols mean?

     (a)   **(b)**   **(c)**   **(d)**   **(e)**

8. What dangers are
    represented here?

     (a)   **(b)**   **(c)**   **(d)**   **(e)**

9. As you complete this quiz, do you know who your nearest first aider is and where
    he or she might be contacted?

10. Where is your nearest fire escape, first aid kit, fire extinguisher and telephone?

Answers

Match of the Day (p.4)

1. (h). 2. (a). 3. (f). 4. (g). 5. (b). 6. (i). 7. (d). 8. (c). 9. (e). 10. (j).

Wordsearch (p.5)

```
Y  E  N  G  I  N  E  E  R  I  N  G  O  P
B  N  A  S  D  H  K  R  I  N  S  N  I  Q
Z  V  D  J  L  I  E  H  E  L  P  I  N  G
C  I  T  S  I  T  R  A  J  P  R  L  F  N
B  R  C  S  H  J  I  C  L  U  Y  L  O  I
S  O  C  L  S  D  P  T  U  T  N  E  R  S
R  N  M  A  E  C  L  I  J  B  H  S  M  I
E  M  V  M  T  I  I  V  A  D  U  B  A  N
B  E  P  I  J  R  S  E  X  Z  W  S  T  A
M  N  H  N  K  T  K  U  N  D  E  R  I  G
U  T  R  A  N  S  P  O  R  T  C  D  O  R
N  A  S  F  N  L  J  Q  C  E  I  W  N  O
A  B  U  I  L  D  I  N  G  M  F  F  M  Z
R  Y  O  A  M  C  S  U  D  G  F  T  I  Y
P  L  W  S  R  E  T  U  P  M  O  C  A  C
```

What do you know about Active and Physical work? (p.6)

1. Caretaker and cleaner. 2. Physics and chemistry. Firefighters use much electrical and mechanical equipment and have to cope with dangerous chemicals. 3. Roughnecks are general labourers, roustabouts help with the drilling procedure. 4. A mobile platform that is used by window cleaners, painters, or glaziers to work outside buildings. 5. (a). An auger is a large drill. 6. (d) the others work at heights. 7. (b). 8. (c). 9. A roadie. 10. Bailiff; a difficult job ensuring that people pay what they owe if they get into debt.

What do you know about Artistic and Creative Work (p.7)

1. (d). This is a sales job with less need to handle the customers. 2. Music, art, or drama therapy. Occupational therapists also use artistic and craft skills. 3. (b). Jiggering is working with flat objects, whereas jollying is working with hollow objects. 4. Print finishers work on a wider range of printed products and have more opportunities for employment. 5. (a). 6. Graphic designers or illustrators. 7. Architecture: Royal Institute of British Architects. 8.(b). 9. True. About 70% work in or around London. 10. Photographer.

Quick Crossword (p.8)

Across: 1. fare. 3. port. 6. plane. 9. plea. 11. unit. 13. sir. 14. pose. 16. sale. 19. cryer. 20. tank. 21. tyre.

Down: 1. flop. 2. rope. 4. open. 5. tint. 7. laser. 8. nurse. 10. leo. 12. ill. 14. post. 15. scan. 17. army. 18. edge.

What do you know about Building & Construction? (p.9)

1. A hod is used by a bricklayer to carry a supply of bricks. 2. A tiler. 3. Four GCSEs (A-C) or S Grades (1-3) including maths, English and a science subject. 4. Banker masons cut and shape the stone, fixer masons assemble the stone in place. 5. Quantity surveyor, estimator. 6. True. 7. (c). A clerk of the works is an experienced builder who inspects work to see that it is being carried out properly and is finished on time. 8. (c). Making timber moulds to cast concrete structures like steps, foundations or bridges. 9. (b). 10. Glazier.

What do you know about Communicating Information and Ideas (p.10)

1. (d). 2. Public Relations Officer. 3. (d). 4. A team of telephonists dealing with customer enquiries or sales. 5. Copy editors work on books, whereas sub-editors work on newspapers and magazines. 6. Two. 7. A Teacher of English as a Foreign Language (TEFL). 8. An area controller. 9. Translator.

Figures of speech (p.11)

1. To share the same problems or predicament. 2. To have a monopoly. 3. To play a junior or lower role. 4. To be auctioned. 5. To clear off. 6. To have a wide range of skills. This may also be an insult implying that none of them are remarkable. 7. To get ready for action. 8. To say something exactly right. 9. To take a well-deserved break. 10. To take action at the right time. 11. To bear the loss or the cost of something. 12. To go out of business. 13. To assume responsibility. 14. To know all the dodges and tricks. 15. To go very close to breaking the law. 16. To talk about one's work. 17. To outwit someone. 18. To be watchful and alert. 19. To behave just like another person. 20. To get one's own back.

Nightmare (p.11)

Had the operator met his end in this manner, we would not know what his dream was about.

Higher Education Quiz (pp. 12 & 13)

I. (c). 2. False. Degree courses are also available in colleges and institutes of higher education as well as some local colleges associated with or affiliated to universities. 3. True. 4. False. If it is received after this date, however, it is up to the institutions whether or not they consider you. 5. False. You can limit your choice to fewer courses than six if you wish. 6. False. The DipHE requires two A-levels/Scottish Higher grades. 7. (b). Contact the college to see if the admissions tutor can still offer you a place. 8. (c) 9. False. 10. (b). one firm offer and one as insurance. 11. True. The admissions staff rely on an application form and a report from the school or referees. 12. False. Means-testing ensures that many students do not pay a contribution. 13. Applications may be made at any stage. 14. True. 25% of the loan is means tested. 15. (a). 16. True. 17. False. It is about two thirds the length. 18. (b). (a) is known as a 'thick' sandwich. 19. False. You may be expected to find your own placement. 20. True. These courses are less popular than subjects such as law, veterinary science or accountancy.

What do you know about Engineering? (p.14)

1. Acoustic, aeronautical, agricultural, automobile, avionic (aircraft). 2. (d) 3. Highways engineer. 4. False. They make special shaping and cutting tools for manufacturing processes. 5. Platers work with thicker and heavier sheets of metal. 6. (a). Designs and looks after medical equipment such as kidney dialysis machines, pacemakers etc. 7. (a), (b) (c) and (d). 8. Electrical engineers are mainly concerned with the supply and use of electricity. Electronic engineers deal with the manufacture and maintenance of things like computers, control systems and telecommunications. 9. Civil engineer. 10. Mechanic.

Newspeak (p.15)

1. People at work: employees. 2. Agreeing. 3. A range or a variety (eg a raft of solutions). Rafts, however, usually sink. 4. Being introduced. 5. Reducing (eg downsizing our human resources). 6. A problem or even a potential disaster. 7. Personal skills such as confidence, leadership etc. 8. An opinion (eg 'What's your take on this?'). 9. A purpose or goal (see p.27). 10. Studying or following. 11. The number of customers or visitors. 12. A major shift or change (eg 'There has been a sea change in our footfall'). 13. Communicating

with other people. 14. Someone who works at a computer from home. 15. A selection (eg a portfolio of soft skills). 16. Temporary promotion. 17. Training. 18. Protecting. 19. Where the action takes place, or the latest approach. 20. A product or service and its public image.

What do you know about Health and Medicine? (p.16)

1. True, but there are not many and they also have other medical qualifications. 2. (b).   3. Chiropractic, osteopath, physiotherapist. 4. A dental technician makes crowns and bridges etc. A dental hygienist gives treatment and advice on avoiding tooth decay and gum disease. 5. A prosthetist. An orthotist fits braces to support parts of the body. 6. (b). 7. Occupational therapist, or, for very young children, a play specialist. 8. They are usually employed in a large organisation or a factory.   9. They treat certain eye problems like squints and 'lazy eye'. 10. Dietitian.

Joined-up talking (p.16)

'In Further Education, after a Certificate of Achievement, I can do a National Vocational Qualification in Information Technology by a Foundation Modern Apprenticeship under a National Training Organisation for my Individual Learning Account.'

What do you know about Helping People? (p.17)

1. Receptionist.   2. True. Not a dying trade but family connections are often very important. 3. (a) Careers advisers. (b) Education welfare officers. (c) Hospital social workers. 4. Childminders care for children up to 12 and are usually self-employed and work in their own homes. Nursery nurses look after younger children, are usually qualified, and work for nurseries, schools, creches, holiday centres etc. 5. (c) would not wear a uniform. 6. False. There are many kinds of counsellors and some are volunteers. 7. Usually works for a large council to see that people of all races, religions and abilities are treated fairly in their employment, housing and community. 8. A chaplain. 9. (c). 10. Warden.

How good a salesperson are you? (pp.18 & 19)

1. (c). If you can discover the reason for the customer's uncertainty, you may be able to offer some useful advice about your other products. 2. (b). Your first goal is to arrange a time when you can discuss the benefits of your product. A sale on the doorstep is very unlikely. 3. (a). There is a chance that the customer may like the models you have in stock. Criticising the customer's choice in (b) is not very tactful and solution (c) shows little imagination. Solution (d) may impress the customer, but you are not running a charity.
4. (d). A leather goods shop usually carries a wide range of goods from simple key fobs to expensive handbags and cases. Your window display should attempt to convey this message to passers by. (a) and (c) distort this message, whereas (b) will discourage many customers from entering the shop. 5. (c) is the best approach. It is similar to (d) but less likely to cause offence. 6. (b). The other solutions are tactless. 7. (a). The other solutions may discourage or irritate the customer. 8. (d) has the edge over (a). Solution (c) could be embarrassing and (b) is just polite small talk.   9. (c). Remember you are trying to sell a television not a repair service as in (d). 10. (b) builds up a relationship with the customer and, having sold the old car, he or she may return to purchase one of your vehicles.

What do you know about Law and Security? (p.20)

1. False. Though some are prison officers, most are recruited through a special scheme. 2. (d). 3. Trading standards officer. 4. True. 5. Environmental health officer. 6. (a). 7. A court clerk is a qualified solicitor or barrister. A court administrative officer requires GCSE/A levels/H grades. 8. False. Some encourage the employment of women on this kind of reception and security work. 9. (d) has increased from 35,000 to 95,000. The others have increased by about 10%. 10. Coastguard.

A to Z (p.21)

Q, U, X, Y and Z may have caused problems. How about quantity surveyor, undertaker, X-ray technician, youth club leader, zoologist?

Ouch! (p.21)

The incorrect items are: 2. address. 3. information . 4. supervisor. 6. committee. 8. applicant. 9. efficiency. 10. temporary. 11. receipt. 13. personnel or personal. 15. benefit. 16. computer. 18. requirement. 19. tenant. 20. occurred. 22. dismiss. 24. consistent.

What's my line? (p.22)

I am a croupier in a gaming club.

What do you know about Leisure, Tourism and Food? (p.22)

1. Management and administrative work in leisure centres, sports centres, gymnasiums, swimming pools, outdoor activities centre etc. Sports coaching and team management. 2. Baker. 3. Tourist guide, tourist information assistant, travel courier. 4. (a). 5. 18 years. 6. False. Most airlines set upper and lower limits. 7. Beauty therapist, manicurist, chiropodist. 8. (d). 9. Porter, room attendant, bar staff, chef, cooks and kitchen staff, nursery nurse, entertainment staff etc. 10. Publican.

What do you know about Media and Entertainment? (p.23)

1. Being out of work. 2. A dancer. 3. Floor manager. 4. (a). 5. (b) and (c). 6. Artistes and Repertoire. 7. Making sure that actors are wearing the same clothes or that the same props are in position from scene to scene. 8. (d). 9. False. There are jobs all over the country: cinemas, nightclubs, theatres, concert halls etc. 10. Musician.

Spot the errors (p.24)

1. Filing cabinets should only be opened one drawer at a time. 2. VDU sticking out over the side of the desk. 3. Notices should not be placed on the back of doors. 4. Fire risk from cigarettte ash in waste paper basket. 5. Incorrect position for lifting heavy objects. Lifter should bend at the knees. 6. Bottle being thrown across the room. 7. Electric kettle could scald someone. 8. Loose wires on the floor. 9. Use a proper stand for working at heights. 10. Fire risk from electric fire.

Odd Links (p.24)

1. Both sit in a rather high chair. 2. Both use hand signals. 3. Both mix fillings. 4. Both work at a keyboard. 5. Both spend a lot of time on their knees. 6. Both use a turntable. 7. Both travel around displaying adverts. 8. Both repair teeth. 9. Both make holes. 10. Both are entitled to take time off work.

What do you know about Office work? (p.25)

1. To cover small expenses or bills. 2. Secretary. Each one has a specialised training. 3. In an organisation awarding grants such as a local council, a charity, the National Lottery or the Arts Council. 4. There is very little difference as nearly all typists now use word processors. 5. (c). 6. Organising board meetings. Taking responsibility for legal documents, the annual budget and internal auditing. 7. Insurance. 8. Legal executive. 9. (c). Arising from the increase in Internet banking services. 10. Secretary.

Interests Quiz (pp.26 & 27)

Scoring: Work across the two pages and add together the three scores in each line. Place the totals in the small boxes. The boxes are in groups of six, so add the six scores together and place them in the larger box. With the help of your six main scores and the following notes, you should be able to see where your interests lie.

1 Practical/Active Preferred by those who enjoy practical activities and like to work with tools, equipment, machinery, or animals. They are usually the kind of people who prefer to get things done rather than just talk about them. Their work may be in fields like engineering, manufacturing, construction and surveying, farming or transport.

2 Enterprising/Persuasive Preferred by those who enjoy activities which give them an opportunity to persuade or organise other people. They often tackle problems with energy and enthusiasm. Their work may be in fields such as management, legal services, sales work, public relations and marketing, or security service.

3 Scientific/Investigative Preferred by those who enjoy scientific activities. They like puzzling out why or how things occur or work. With academic qualifications, their work could be in scientific, technical, or medical research.

4 Clerical/Administrative Preferred by those who enjoy activities which involve checking or calculating facts or figures. They are often well organised and tidy minded. Their work could be in finance, management support, office work, library work, computers, or transport administration.

5 Artistic/Creative Preferred by those who like art and design, playing music, or writing. They often enjoy imaginative activities. With talents their work could be in art and design, hairdressing, entertainment, journalism, photography, etc. Without talent or contacts they meet lots of new friends in the dole queue.

6 Social/Supportive Preferred by those who are interested in work of a caring nature. They often enjoy participating in community service activities. Their work could be in community services, nursing and the therapies, teaching, or child care.

Interest combinations: Perhaps two areas show up in your scores. If so, here are some interpretations based on many years of research into people's interests.

Practical and scientific. An interest in research and development.
Practical and artistic. An interest in the man-made environment.
Scientific and artistic. An interest in intellectual pursuits, an 'ideas' person.
Scientific and social. Often associated with a strong interest in medical matters.
Scientific and clerical. An interest in mathematics, statistics, and computers.
Artistic and social. An interest in cultural activities. Not aggressive or assertive.
Artistic and enterprising. An outgoing and attention-seeking personality.
Social and enterprising. A strong interest in people. Unhappy if isolated.
Social and clerical. Often the pattern of helpful and sensitive administrators.
Enterprising and clerical. An interest in business, sales, and administration.
Enterprising and practical. Tough-minded. May run a small practical business.
Clerical and practical. Likes a clearly defined task and stays in the background.

Here is a key to the 36 scores which you obtained from adding up three items in a row: Your scores may help to identify a particular kind of interest within the six general fields described earlier.

1. agriculture	13. medical science	25. music
2. animals	14. veterinary science	26. entertainment
3. surveying	15. plant research	27. graphics
4. transport	16. the environment	28. design
5. construction	17. technology	29. crafts
6. manufacturing	18. human behaviour	30. writing
7. negotiating	19. costing	31. disabled people
8. selling objects	20. finance	32. medical care
9. selling services	21. statistics	33. therapy
10. management	22. documentation	34. children
11. law and order	23. files and records	35. education
12. communicating	24. work with plans	36. guidance

Circled words. Take a closer look at the words which you circled as they may reveal some interesting things about you. Did you mainly select verbs, objects, or work environments? Can you find any other links between your words? Share your selection with a friend. What does he or she make of them?

What do you know about Organising Information and People? (p.28)

1. (b). 2. Master in Business Administration. 3. False, they are also employed by private hospitals. 4. (c). 5. These are regiments that support the Combat Arms, eg Royal Engineers or the Intelligence Corps. 6. True, there are also dual certificate officers. 7. In a surgery. 8. A hammer used by a judge, an auctioneer, or a toastmaster to attract attention. 9. Distribution (or Transport) manager. 10. Administrator.

Puzzler 1. (p.29)

It was investigating alcohol abuse and related diseases.

What do you know about Scientific and Technical work? (p.29)

1. Mathematics. 2. (a). 3. Non-destructive testing. 4. Astronomy, meteorology, astrophysics, aeronautical science, space exploration, traditional navigation, astrology. 5. Food scientists study the chemistry and biology of food, whereas food technologists find new ways of making food products. 6. Research and Development. 7. Solving crimes and investigating accidents. 8. All could be involved in this type of work. 9. Quality control inspector. 10. Biologist.

Crossword (p.30)

Across: 6. photographer. 8. sellers. 9. corps. 10. edit. 12. dancer. 14. spoil. 15. guests. 16. heal. 19. resit. 21. rolling. 22. demonstrator.
Down: 1. coal mine. 2. money. 3. press. 4. special. 5. gear. 6. passengers. 7. astrologer. 11. BPS. (British Psychological Society). 12. dig. 13. chemists. 14. station. 17. crash. 18. clerk. 20. sued.

What do you know about Selling and Shopwork? (p.31)

1. (c). 2. An antique dealer or a furniture dealer. Distressed means the item has been deliberately marked or damaged to make it appear older. 3. Airport, rail terminal, seaport, garage, large hotel, etc. 4. (c). A shelf that is at eye level and which attracts the attention of customers. 5. In an estate agency. 6. Someone who buys the right to run a business using the franchiser's name, trademark and business system. 7. Buying goods or services through the internet. In 2000 it accounted for 5% of retail sales. 8. Calling on a customer without having first made an appointment. 9. (b) commercial, (d) receipt, (f) advertisement.
10. Merchandiser.

Puzzler 2. (p.31)

(d), but this is less true today with the growth of supermarkets and the decline of small shops.

What do you know about Environmental work? (p.32)

1. (d). 2. Rangers perform practical tasks in nature reserves and national parks. Countryside officers promote conservation and enforce laws that protect the countryside. 3. (a). 4. Developing and maintaining sports grounds and recreational areas. 5. A digging machine used by gardeners, landscapers and farmers for turning over soil and rough ground. 6. For their appearance and contribution to the environment. 7. Solar, water or wind power. 8. (c). 9. Sewage is human waste whereas sewerage is the system of transferring or draining it. 10. Landscaper.

Interview Quiz.(p.33)

The correct order is: spare, there, facts, relax, called, mind, kind, smart, start, questions, flow, No, Smiths, crisps, ask, training, last, for, door, applied, part, manager, start, knew, interview.

What do you know about Transport and Driving? (p.34)

1. (d). 2. patient, reliable, discrete, self-defence, smart appearance, observant.
3. Information about routes through, and places in, a large city. 4. False. Some are employed by local councils. 5. (a) does not need to steer. 6. A car dealer (or used-vehicle redistribution consultant!) for checking on vehicle prices. 7. (b). Under the Young Drivers' Scheme you can train to drive certain vehicles. 8. (c). 9. No. 10. Helicopter.

Puzzler 3. (p.34)

At work, they usually wear something on their head.

Yesterday's jobs (p.35)

1. A bodkin was used by a basket weaver to make holes. 2. A gag was used by a vet to keep an animal's mouth open whilst administering medicine. 3. A yoke was used by a farmhand to carry pails of milk.

4. A gripping key was used by a dentist to extract teeth. 5. A foot plate was used by a gardener to protect footwear when digging. 6. A traveller was used by a wheelwright to measure the circumference of a wheel. 7. A bottomer was used by a bodger (chairmaker) to shape the seat of a chair. 8. A block was used by a milliner to shape straw hats. 9. A signal stone was placed by a baker in an oven and turned white when the heat was right for baking. 10. A stuffing iron was used by a saddler for filling saddles with straw.

What do you know about work with Animals? (p.36)

1. Dog groomer, dog beautician, poodle clipper. 2. (c). 3. True. 4. Jumping and hurdling. 5. False. Racing greyhounds are exercised by walking. 6. (d). 7. Pest controller or pest control technician. 8. Fish farmer. 9. Police, Customs and Excise, Army, Royal Air Force, Security organisations. 10. Stablehand.

Rights and Responsibilities (p.37)

The incorrect items are 4, 14 (only employees who have worked for two years beyond the age of 20 are entitled to redundancy payments), 17, and 20 (workers are only required to obey lawful commands). Note that some of the rights listed do not apply to casual, freelance or temporary workers, and items 9 and 10 do not apply to all jobs - exceptions are made in certain sea-going, transport, security, medical and continuous process occupations.

What do you know about work with Computers? (p.38)

1. Equipment like computers, drives, keyboards, printers etc. 2. To crash. 3. Information Technology. 4. (c). 5. A bug is a program error, whereas a virus is designed to cause some kind of failure and can spread from one computer to another. 6. A systems analyst or a systems integrator. 7. Database. 8. Headaches, migraine, dizziness, sore eyes, sore throat, nausea, stiff neck, repetitive strain injury. 9. Both will design websites, but a webmaster is responsible for running them on the internet. 10. Helpdesk.

Job Satisfactions (p.39)

	The top five	The bottom five
Men:	6. 8. 18. 4. 9.	7. 3. 13. 20. 21.
Women:	8. 6. 18. 17. 9.	3. 7. 2. 19. 21.

What do you know about work with Numbers? (p.40)

1. Payroll clerks. 2. Towards the end of the financial year (early April). 3. A bursar. 4. (b). 5. (a). 6. In the foreign exchange section of a bank. 7. (d). 8. For a local council collecting council taxes and business rates. 9. Auditor. 10. Statistician.

What do you know about working with your Hands? (p.41)

1. (d). 2. (c) works in a foundry, (a) and (b) are found in the clothing trade. 3. False. An ear for tone and pitch is more important. 4. (b). A glory hole is a small furnace, a blowpipe is used by a glassblower, and a servitor is a person who shapes and finishes glass articles. 5. French polishing. 6. A blacksmith. 7. (a). 8. (b). A kneekicker is used to stretch the carpet taut, and grippers secure the carpet around skirting boards and stairs. 9. A saddler. 10. Upholsterer.

Survival (p.42)

1. (b). Never burst blisters and forget about grease. Any dressing should be applied lightly. 2. (d). 3. (a) and check that she can breathe. Then (c) but avoid (b). 4. (c). 5. A is for airway - is it open and clear? B is for breathing. C is for circulation - is there a pulse?. 6. Check for broken glass. A wound to yourself could increase the risk of any cross-infection. 7. (a) Do not extinguish fire with water. (b) Do not drink this water. (c) Do not enter. (d) Do not smoke. (e) Do not use a naked flame. 8. (a) electricity cable. (b) slippery floor. (c) toxic substance. (d) explosive substance. (e) inflammable.